SIMON AND SCHUSTER BOOKS FOR YOUNG READERS
Simon & Schuster Building
Rockefeller Center
1230 Avenue of the Americas
New York, New York 10020

10 9 8 7 6 5 4 3 2 1
10 9 8 7 6 5 4 3 2 1 (Pbk)
Library of Congress Cataloging-in-Publication Data
Silverman, Maida. Dinosaur babies. Summary: Discusses the physical characteristics, habits, and natural environment of nine different dinosaurs. 1. Dinosaurs—Juvenile literature. [1. Dinosaurs] I. Inouye, Carol. II. Title.   QE862.D5S5 1988   567.9'1   88-4690   ISBN 0-671-65897-2   ISBN 0-671-69438-3 (Pbk)

DINOSAUR BABIES

BY MAIDA SILVERMAN
ILLUSTRATED BY CAROL INOUYE

SIMON AND SCHUSTER BOOKS FOR YOUNG READERS
PUBLISHED BY SIMON & SCHUSTER INC., NEW YORK

Millions of years ago, our planet was very different than it is now. The climate was hot and moist. Volcanos belched fire, smoke and melted rock into the air. Oceans were warm and shallow. Trees with huge, spiky leaves grew in coastal forests. Giant ferns grew in swampy places. Land, sea and air swarmed with fantastic creatures in all shapes and sizes. This was the world of the dinosaurs. They lived on earth for almost 200 million years, and died out millions of years before the first humans were born.

In 1841 a scientist, Dr. Richard Owen, formed the word *dinosaur* from two Greek words that meant "terrible lizard." Some dinosaurs really were terrible—huge creatures with long, sharp teeth and claws. They hunted and ate other dinosaurs. But many dinosaurs were gentle. They ate leaves, fruit and berries. Some dinosaurs were taller than a three-storey house. Others were as small as a chicken.

Dinosaurs laid eggs and baby dinosaurs hatched from them. When baby dinosaur bones were first found, people supposed they were a new type of small dinosaur. Now scientists know they are really fossils of baby dinosaurs. Thousands of adult dinosaur bones have been discovered, but fossils of baby and

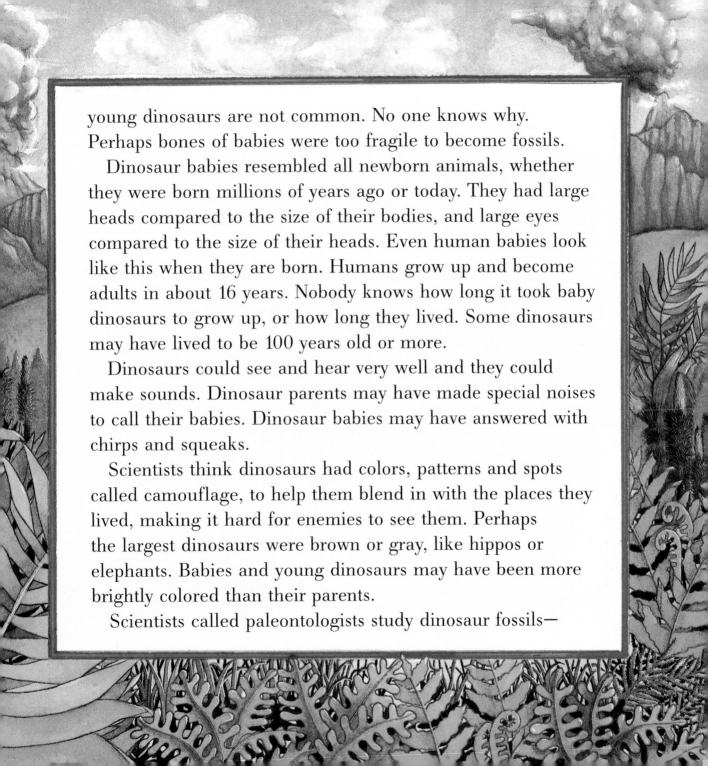

young dinosaurs are not common. No one knows why. Perhaps bones of babies were too fragile to become fossils.

Dinosaur babies resembled all newborn animals, whether they were born millions of years ago or today. They had large heads compared to the size of their bodies, and large eyes compared to the size of their heads. Even human babies look like this when they are born. Humans grow up and become adults in about 16 years. Nobody knows how long it took baby dinosaurs to grow up, or how long they lived. Some dinosaurs may have lived to be 100 years old or more.

Dinosaurs could see and hear very well and they could make sounds. Dinosaur parents may have made special noises to call their babies. Dinosaur babies may have answered with chirps and squeaks.

Scientists think dinosaurs had colors, patterns and spots called camouflage, to help them blend in with the places they lived, making it hard for enemies to see them. Perhaps the largest dinosaurs were brown or gray, like hippos or elephants. Babies and young dinosaurs may have been more brightly colored than their parents.

Scientists called paleontologists study dinosaur fossils—

bones, footprints, eggs and other remains. They examine the rocks fossils are found in. They study fossils of all kinds of plants and creatures that lived millions of years past. From these studies, we learn about dinosaurs, dinosaur babies and how they might have lived.

We also learn about dinosaurs by studying how living animals who resemble dinosaurs behave. Perhaps dinosaur mothers behaved like crocodiles, their closest reptile relatives. Scientists think the eggs of dinosaurs were most likely the same color as today's reptiles—white. Large dinosaurs may have behaved like elephants in some ways. Perhaps some dinosaurs behaved like certain birds.

No one has ever seen a dinosaur and no one ever will. Were there dinosaurs who gave birth to live babies? Did dinosaur babies play with each other? Did any dinosaur mothers have pouches like kangaroos to carry their babies in? Could a mother dinosaur pick up her baby by the scruff of its neck and carry it like mother cats carry kittens? Scientists aren't yet able to say yes or no to any of these questions. Perhaps some day they will.

ALLOSAURUS

AL-uh-sawr-us

Allosaurs were very fierce dinosaurs. Scientists call them "the tigers of their time." The mother Allosaur was gigantic—as big as an animal can grow to be and still run around on two hind legs. Her head was huge and her jaw was filled with long, sharp teeth. She had powerful claws on each small, three-fingered hand. Allosaurs hunted other dinosaurs and ate them. They also may have been scavengers, eating animals that had died.

The mother Allosaur may have cared for her babies as mother crocodiles do today. After laying her eggs in a shallow nest of soft earth, the Allosaur mother stood guard, protecting her eggs from dinosaurs that liked to eat them.

After a while, she heard small sounds coming from the earth-covered nest. The sounds were made by babies still inside the eggs, and meant they were ready to hatch. Quickly but carefully, she dug earth away from the eggs. With her big front tooth, she helped the babies by gently cutting the shells open. A few babies may have hatched by themselves. Soon, many baby Allosaurs were running around. The mother Allosaur was careful not to step on any of them.

Scientists digging in Utah found sixty Allosaurs of different ages and sizes all in one place. Perhaps this was a group of Allosaur parents and youngsters who lived together.

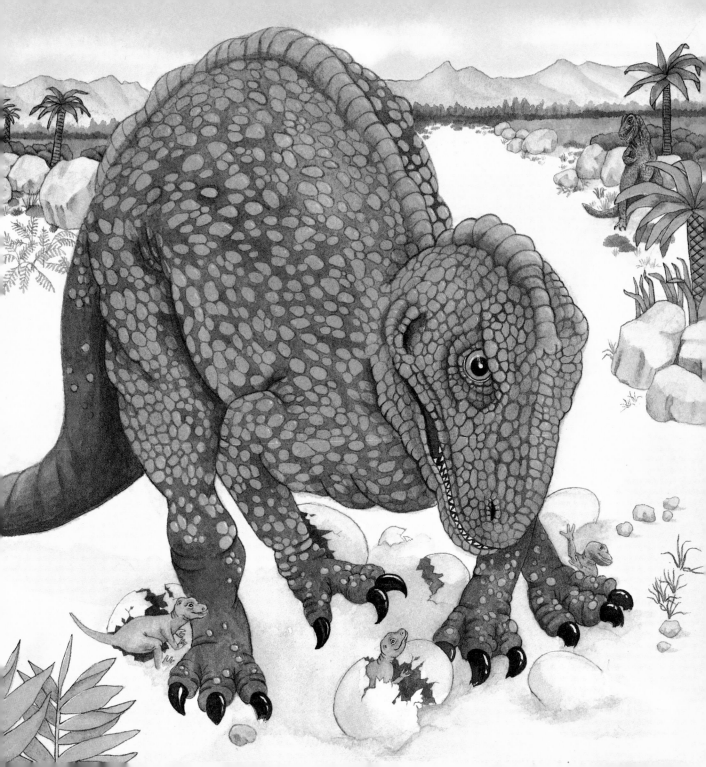

BRACHIOSAURUS

BRAK-ee-uh-sawr-us

Brachiosaurus was one of the largest animals ever to walk the earth. One Brachiosaur weighed more than twenty elephants and its neck was twice as long as a giraffe's. Huge but gentle, Brachiosaurs moved peacefully through the highland pine forests, nibbling from treetops.

The mother Brachiosaurus may have laid her eggs as giant turtles do today. She found a warm, sandy spot, somewhere between the forest and the sea. She dug and turned around and around in the sand to make a large, shallow nest.

From a special place under her tail called a vent, large, round eggs dropped into the nest. Mother Brachiosaur used her tail to cover the eggs with sand, hiding them completely. Then she walked away, never to return.

The sand protected the eggs from animals that liked to eat them, and kept them warm until they hatched. Weeks later, tiny Brachiosaurs climbed out of the nest and scurried into the nearby forest to hide. They probably ate insects, tiny animals and low-growing plants. As they grew bigger, they began to eat the kinds of plants adult Brachiosaurs ate.

CAMARASAURUS

KAM-uh-ruh-sawr-us

Camarasaurs were huge, plant-eating dinosaurs with long necks and tails. They had large eyes and their teeth—40 of them—looked like enormous flat spoons. Camarasaur babies had large eyes, but short tails and necks. They traveled in herds, like elephants. Babies and youngsters traveled with the herd for protection. A Camarasaur mother or father could

jump on an enemy with its large front feet, or lash it with its powerful tail.

Some scientists think that Camarasaurs had elephant-like trunks. A mother Camarasaur could have used her trunk to pull leaves from treetops for her babies to eat. Perhaps baby Camarasaurs used their trunks to playfully spray each other with water.

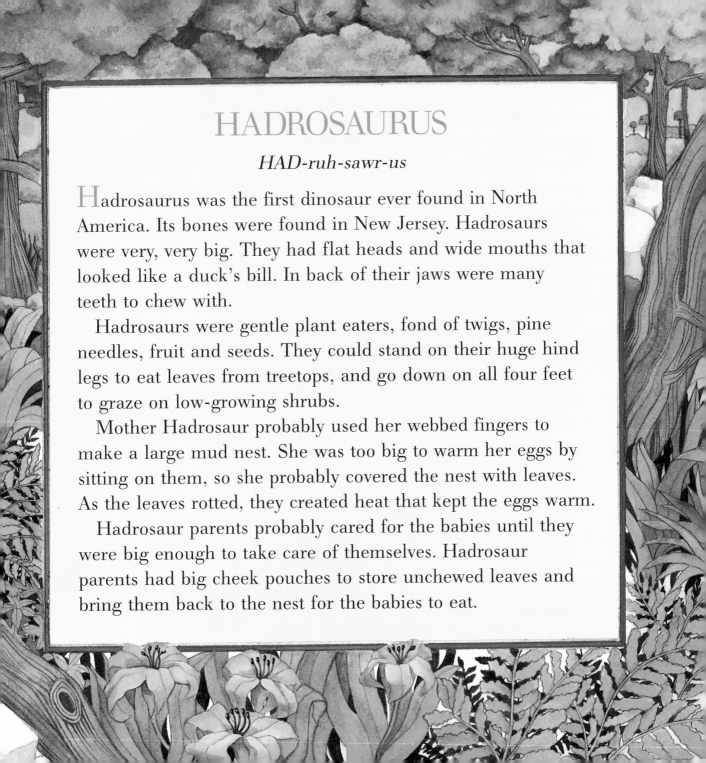

HADROSAURUS

HAD-ruh-sawr-us

Hadrosaurus was the first dinosaur ever found in North America. Its bones were found in New Jersey. Hadrosaurs were very, very big. They had flat heads and wide mouths that looked like a duck's bill. In back of their jaws were many teeth to chew with.

Hadrosaurs were gentle plant eaters, fond of twigs, pine needles, fruit and seeds. They could stand on their huge hind legs to eat leaves from treetops, and go down on all four feet to graze on low-growing shrubs.

Mother Hadrosaur probably used her webbed fingers to make a large mud nest. She was too big to warm her eggs by sitting on them, so she probably covered the nest with leaves. As the leaves rotted, they created heat that kept the eggs warm.

Hadrosaur parents probably cared for the babies until they were big enough to take care of themselves. Hadrosaur parents had big cheek pouches to store unchewed leaves and bring them back to the nest for the babies to eat.

MAIASAURA

mah-ee-ah-SAWR-uh

In 1978, scientists digging for fossils in Montana made an important discovery—fifteen dinosaur babies, the first ever found in a nest. Eventually, the scientists found a colony of more than sixty dinosaurs of all ages and sizes. Until this discovery, no one thought dinosaurs cared for their babies. Scientists named the dinosaur *Maiasaurus*, which means "good mother lizard." Maiasaurs were large, with long, straight

duck-like bills and a short, bony spike between the eyes.

Maiasaur nests were hollowed-out mud domes made in high, dry pine woods, spaced one dinosaur-length apart. There were several at the site. Some babies were very small, about 4 weeks old. Others were older and bigger. The mother Maiasaur brought pine needles, twigs, berries and fruit back to her nest for the babies to eat. The father Maiasaur stood guard while she was away. Both parents may have led bigger Maiasaur youngsters to the forests to graze.

MUSSAURUS

moo-SAWR-us

Mussaurus babies are the smallest dinosaurs ever found. A nest with three tiny babies, only just hatched, was discovered in Chile, in South America. One baby was not much larger than a mouse. It fit easily into a person's two cupped hands. Scientists also found two Mussaur eggs. They were tiny too— the size of a twenty-five cent piece.

No one knows how big Mussaurus parents were. They might have been as large as an alligator, or as small as a robin. The mother Mussaur may have kept her nest of eggs warm by sitting on them until the babies hatched.

STRUTHIOMIMUS

strooth-ee-uh-MY-mus

Struthiomimus means "ostrich mimic." This dinosaur did look very much like an ostrich. Ostriches have wings, but they cannot fly. Struthiomimus did not have wings. It had long arms with powerful claws, strong legs and a long tail. Its head was small, with big eyes and a beaked mouth. Scientists think

it may have been very intelligent. The parents may have behaved like today's ostriches in the way they laid eggs and cared for babies.

Mothers laid eggs in a shallow nest lined with twigs and dry leaves hidden behind trees and bushes. More than one mother may have shared the same nest. The father Struthiomimus stood guard, ready to chase away dinosaurs that liked to eat eggs. He led the babies away to find food, and watched over them while they caught insects to eat.

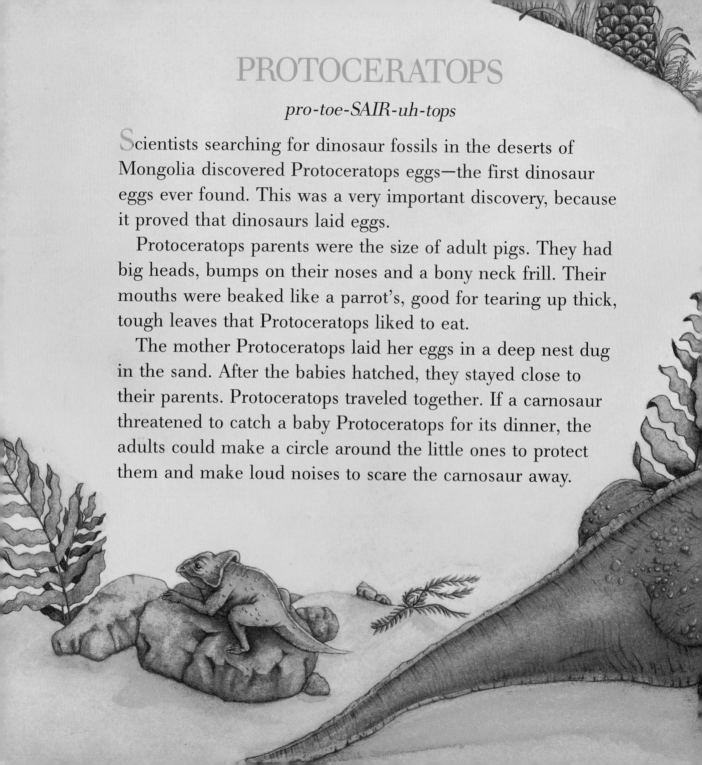

PROTOCERATOPS

pro-toe-SAIR-uh-tops

Scientists searching for dinosaur fossils in the deserts of Mongolia discovered Protoceratops eggs—the first dinosaur eggs ever found. This was a very important discovery, because it proved that dinosaurs laid eggs.

Protoceratops parents were the size of adult pigs. They had big heads, bumps on their noses and a bony neck frill. Their mouths were beaked like a parrot's, good for tearing up thick, tough leaves that Protoceratops liked to eat.

The mother Protoceratops laid her eggs in a deep nest dug in the sand. After the babies hatched, they stayed close to their parents. Protoceratops traveled together. If a carnosaur threatened to catch a baby Protoceratops for its dinner, the adults could make a circle around the little ones to protect them and make loud noises to scare the carnosaur away.

ARCHAEOPTERYX

ar-kee-OP-ter-ix

Archaeopteryx, which means "ancient feather wing," was the earliest bird. It had the skeleton of a dinosaur, but it had a wishbone, feathers and wings, like a bird. On each wing was a grasping, three-clawed hand. Archaeopteryx had a long, bony tail and skinny jaws lined with tiny teeth.

Archaeopteryx may not have flown very well—its bones and muscles were not strong enough. It may have climbed up into trees with its clawed wings and feet and used its wings to glide.

No one really knows how Archaeopteryx parents and babies behaved, but there is a clue. Along the banks of the Amazon River, deep in the jungles of South America, lives a bird called the Hoatzin (ho-AT-zin). Babies hatch with three claws on each wing and climb through trees by grasping branches with their clawed wings and feet. When they grow up, the wing claws fall off.

The mother Archaeopteryx may have built her nest in a tree like a Hoatzin does. It would have been safer than a nest on the ground. Perhaps she sat on her eggs, warming them with her feathers until they hatched. The father Archaeopteryx

may have brought insects for the babies to eat. The young Archaeopteryx could have learned how to use their wings by watching their parents glide.

Some scientists believe birds are descended from dinosaurs. Others think birds really *are* dinosaurs that survived long after all the others disappeared.